The Most Beautiful Cookie in the World

It was a hopeless endeavor, Ginger knew. She had not caught as much as a glimpse of her brother in three days, and yet now she was tasked with finding the dolt—and all by herself, no less! He was likely in Kansas, or India, or some such place; but no, Mr. Theo had insisted that the scallywag would not exit the borders of Sprinkleton. She dared not question the man's wisdom (not audibly, at least), but she wondered how anyone could be sure of her brother's whereabouts. Who could hope to fathom the mind of a rogue gingerbread man with a penchant for wicked deeds?

Yes, her brother (Molasses was his name) was a gingerbread man, and *she* was a gingerbread woman. And yes, she was quite aware that cookies did not have the tendency to think, speak, or move—but she could do all three. It was not she and her brother who had given themselves life, but Mr. Theo, the ostensibly sage man who had sent her on this fool's errand. Mr. Theo had lived in Sprinkleton for an eternity and was well-beloved by its five dozen or so denizens. The man was a baker by profession, and for the past several decades, on Christmas Eve, he had provided countless cookies for the families at no cost and with only one rule: each family must eat their cookies on Christmas Day, no sooner. Every year he could be seen riding his motorized bike along the cobbled streets, tiered trays of goodies nestled securely in his apple-red sidecar, his salt-and-pepper beard undulating in the wind like the waves of the sea. At each home he would stop for a brief chat and, more importantly, for the delivery of the morsels. Then he would be off to the next house with many a cheerful laugh, Sprinkleton's very own Santa Claus—slightly slimmer but no less jolly.

The love that Mr. Theo poured into every batch of baked goods was evident to all. According to the man himself, he had done nothing different with the latest batch of cookies he had prepared, but the love he had felt for his craft and the townspeople had overflowed and somehow enlivened the gingerbread batter. When the cookies had come out of the oven, he had been shocked to see two of them stand upright and begin to walk around. Thus Ginger's consciousness had begun, though her maker had not named her right then and there; he had taken a moment to try and avoid fainting (usually a good idea), and another moment to examine his cup of eggnog for signs of a hallucinogen (there was no such drug to be found). After another minute of mild panic, wonder, and acceptance, he had scooped up the cookies into his hands and greeted them with understandable trepidation. To her own surprise, Ginger and her brother, still mouthless, had managed to grunt a shy "hello" in response. She had then half-noticed a man hovering in the background before grumbling to himself and exiting the baker's house. An unimportant detail, she had thought at the time. How very wrong she had been.

Focus, Ginger, focus! she chided herself, trying to think less about her last few days with her brother and more about the task at hand. She released a sigh—one that was far too deep and melancholy for such a delectable cookie—and gently pushed ajar the cupboard door she had been hiding behind. There had been the patter of footsteps and the glowing of overhead lights a minute or so earlier, but she could now see that the humans had turned in for the night. The only source of luminescence was beyond the kitchen, out in the living room; an absurdly large Christmas tree was festooned with silver-white ornaments, and around it also were draped bright yellow, blue, red, and white string lights. The radiance of those lights graced every corner of the room, illuminating the mountain of presents around the tree, the Santa Claus statuettes keeping guard on tabletops, the family's hideous furniture (who bought orange couches, anyway?), a stool topped with a plate of store-bought cookies for Santa, and even the wreath-bedecked front door some distance away. Ginger, ever the adorer of bright and pretty things, shut the cabinet silently behind her and made a mad dash across the kitchen tile, over the plush carpet of the living room, and to the base of the presents. There she gazed at the tree in awe, and there she espied her reflection in one of the spherical white ornaments.

Ginger was, without a doubt and certainly without bias, the most beautiful cookie in the world. Her pretty dress was delineated by flowy white frosting just above her legs and above her arms, and two red candies served as its buttons. A deep green bow rested on the left side of her head at a crooked angle, her dark cream eyes stared back at her, and her perpetual smile stretched not far below. Mr. Theo had also been so kind as to demarcate little icing-shoes at the bottom of her legs which, in her most humble opinion, tidied up the ensemble perfectly. She desperately tried to ignore the fact that her brother resembled her in pretty much every way except for the bow and the dress. That lummox was always trying to copy her style.

After recalling the dangers of narcissism, Ginger tore herself away from her makeshift mirror and turned her attention to her brother's whereabouts. Doubt swept through her again. It was like looking for a needle in a haystack, but at least needles did not have minds of their own. And yet Mr. Theo had said something to her, she recalled. What was it again? "You and your brother are of the same batch," the man had told her. "In many ways, you are alike. You can surely think the way he thinks if you so desire. Indeed, there is no one more qualified for this mission than you, Ginger. I entrust it—him—to your capable hands. Bring him home." She appreciated his vote of confidence, but she was not so sure she could think like her brother since his recent change. He was not the same cookie he used to be.

  No excuses, Ginger, she chided herself again. *All you can do is try. Now let's get going. Where would Molasses be if he were in this house right now?* She gazed first to the island in the center of the kitchen, on which a tin container of Mr. Theo's famous cookies sat; she could tell the tin was unopened, as the sticker that the man used to seal every container remained intact. Next, she turned her eyes back across the carpet and kitchen tile to the cupboard she had exited. *Molasses is not a* total *buffoon. He would be surveying the territory, scouting it out to ensure that the coast is clear. And he would be doing that from a safe place—a place where no one could spot him. That means either way up high or way down low. Let's check out the bottom cupboards first.*

  She hobbled back into the kitchen and proceeded to open the cabinet doors just a crack so she could quickly determine whether any of her brother's crumbs had been left behind in his travels. It was a shame that she could rely only on her sight, but as is well-known, gingerbread cookies generally do not possess noses, because that would look very odd indeed, and no one likes to chomp down on a cookie with a freakish appearance. She, too, had no nose to speak of—so she looked, and she looked, and she looked, and she could not find a single brown crumb in five different cabinets. As she had thought before, it was likely that Molasses was moseying about inside one of the fourteen other homes of Sprinkleton, far away from her. She was ready to move on to the upper cabinets when she spotted one final cupboard door beside the fridge off to her right. There stood a thin cabinet, probably not spacious enough to serve as a respectable refuge. But it could not be ignored; she could leave no stone unturned.

  To Ginger's surprise, the cabinet was empty, devoid of both kitchenware and crumbs. It was altogether unimpressive, but there was one unique feature that Ginger found interesting: a cord, its origin unknown, slithered into the cabinet through a hole on the right side and out through a hole in the back wall. Ginger tiptoed—as well as a toeless cookie *can* tiptoe, at any rate—deeper into the space and observed that the cord on the right seemed to connect to the refrigerator. *The perfect hiding spot,* she thought. *If Molasses were here, he could move in and out of the kitchen at his leisure, retreating behind the cabinets any time he wanted. If I were in his shoes, this would be my base of operations. But you know what they say about assumptions. Let's see what awaits me behind the cabinet....*

In utter silence, she hopped and seized the cord mid-flight, then shimmied toward the back wall with grunts that betrayed her lack of athleticism. She managed to hang on just long enough to inch herself over the rim of the hole, but by then her arms were exhausted, and the last crumb of her strength was spent. With a yelp she released the cord and plunged into a darkness so deep that she could not see her flailing arms—nor could she see the ground when she landed upon it a second later. Internally admitting that she had been slightly overdramatic, she allowed herself a moment to recuperate and to confirm that she still bore all four limbs. Satisfied, she pressed on into the thick darkness ahead.

So heavy was the quiet of night that she could audibly hear her every thought and breath. Thankfully, the darkness around her was brightening moment by moment as her frosting-eyes adjusted—and truly, there appeared to be nothing of note in the space save an unpainted wall and a thick carpet of dust. Once she was able to see more clearly, she also observed that there were little footprints skirting the baseboard to the right, but it was impossible to determine if they belonged to her brother in the dim light. Nonetheless, she figured that it would be safest to follow the signs of former traffic, so she took to the footpath and traced the baseboard with one arm as she went along. After a minute or so, she could see that the prints turned to the right into an illuminated nook; she also could have sworn that she heard some sort of *chatter* coming from within! Was it Molasses, speaking to himself and ruminating about his next plan of attack? Or had he stumbled upon a co-conspirator with whom he was presently strategizing? Inspired, Ginger changed her pace to a sprint and made for the nook ahead.

She was about to turn the corner and shout, "Found you!" when a flash of yellow suddenly appeared and smashed her right in the face. She knew that something was wrong when she saw her legs stretching out before her and the black of the ceiling looming far above. The next moment she felt the back of her head hit the floor, and a darkness thicker than that which she had theretofore experienced rushed upon her.

CHAPTER 2
The Colony Behind the Cabinets

When Ginger awoke, she could make very little sense of her surroundings. The first thing she noticed was a row of potatoes lining the base of a nearby wall, a single screw protruding from each one; around each screw a wire was wrapped tautly, and each wire was connected to a single string lightbulb. The bulbs, glowing gold and white, were decorating what seemed to be a makeshift Christmas tree, which itself was comprised of a pincushion stuffed full of pine needles. Opposite the wall was a set of stairs that led to the entrance of the nook, where she had been struck by an unknown enemy. Surrounding the Christmas tree was a square pavilion carpeted with threads of various materials; Ginger could tell that there were bits of blanket, pillow, and even paper on the ground. Chunks of cheese, ranging in color from white to yellow to orange, had been stacked beside dollops of peanut butter against the walls to her right and left. She found it odd that she was lying on her back with large staples holding her to the floor by her arms and legs, and odder still that there were more than a dozen mice hovering around her, staring at her as if she were some sort of Martian cookie (which, she had been told, was a real thing).

The mice appeared to be startled by her abrupt movements, and several of them hopped back and chattered to one another. Ginger could not blame them, really. She had given her creator a near heart attack, after all, and she was not so sure mice had the fortitude of a human.

"I *told* you she could move, Horace!" cried one of the critters with a feminine voice, her green dress—fashioned from the label of a tuna can—whipping around her. "She's just like the other one! She's a monster!"

"Thanks a bunch, Ingrid," retorted another mouse, whom Ginger gathered was Horace. He wore a cardboard shirt tied together with string. "Now she knows my name."

Ingrid's paws flew to her face. "Now she knows *my* name!"

Ginger grunted and glanced from face to face. "What happened? What are you lot going to do to me?"

"The cookie *talks*?" Ingrid almost swooned. "It really *is* the end!"

"Oh, come on, Ingrid," Horace muttered. He leaned on a dried cherry stem that served as a cane. "She's obv'sly disoriented, seeing how Arthur knocked her out cold with that block of gouda. Great work, Arthur."

Arthur took a bow, and many of his peers nearby rolled their eyes.

"And another thing!" Horace continued. "We've got her snug as a bug on our rug due to our most excellent staple-cuffs; she's not gettin' out any time soon."

Ginger, ever the polite cookie and being loath to interrupt, raised her arm to ask a question. The instant she lifted her arm, the staple was pried from the ground and thrown clear across the room. "Oh, look at that!" she exclaimed. "Oops."

Ingrid glared at Horace. "Most excellent staple-cuffs? At this rate she'll be out of there before you can say, 'Cheddar.' We've tried to take care of the problem ourselves, but we just don't have the brains. I need to tell the King, STAT."

"The King?" Horace shook his head. "He don't need to be troubled by something so small as this, 'specially with all that he has on his mind these days."

But Ingrid was already on her way. She marched past the makeshift Christmas tree, past the line of potatoes, and over to a panel of wood that covered part of the back wall. After rapping against the door with a very intricate knock, she waited. Ginger took the opportunity to examine her surroundings more carefully in case she needed to make a hasty escape. By now each mouse was engaged in deep conversation with his neighbor, unfazed, apparently, by the likelihood that their captive could free herself from her restraints. She could use their naivete to her advantage, dash downstairs, and find another cord to climb her way out of the wall void. But based on the little she knew about mice, she was not so confident that she could outrun them; and if she proved too much trouble and their curiosity faded, what was to stop them from turning her into a five-course meal? She was pretty sure mice would eat just about anything!

She also thought it might be worthwhile to stick around, as one of her captors—Ingrid—had mentioned that there was "the other one" besides her. Had they seen Molasses? Had he done something to spook or harm them, which was why they had resorted to knocking her unconscious instead of hailing her and exchanging pleasantries? Scanning the homemade carpet around her, she saw no sign of her brother's crumbs. No, he had not been here, but maybe he had been nearby.

After what seemed like an eternity, Ingrid returned to the group and motioned toward the door with her head. "The King wants to speak to our guest. Horace, Arthur, will you get her up? Bring her into the throne room and leave her. The King will talk to her alone."

"A—alone?" asked Arthur in a slow, dopey voice. "Is—is that a good idea?"

"That's what he said," replied Ingrid with a shrug. "I don't like it, either. I think she's dangerous. But I'm not top-mouse here."

Horace sighed and, along with Arthur, tugged the remaining staples from Ginger's limbs. They pulled her up and proceeded to direct her to the wood slat behind the small mountain of potatoes. The chatter among the mice now became more animated; Ginger surmised that it was uncommon for a foreigner to be allowed a face-to-face dialogue with their leader. She went willingly with her guides but feared what manner of king she was soon to meet. Was he just and kind and inviting, or was he rash and quick-tempered and unwelcoming? Would she be accepted by him into the rodent community, or would she be executed for trespassing? She entertained one final moment's thought of fleeing, but once she had walked past the pincushion tree, she knew that it was too late to turn back.

The male mice lifted the wood slat for her and beckoned her inside. She inclined her head to each of them in turn and entered the room; the door slammed to the ground right behind her. What she saw when she peered ahead was something that failed to meet her every expectation of what a king's throne room *should* be. She had always imagined a lengthy, soft red carpet extending from entrance to throne, purple thread woven into its edges; she had imagined sturdy pillars layered with gold standing every few steps, supporting a roof emblazoned with mesmerizing artwork; she had hoped to see braziers fashioned after mythological creatures such as dragons, smoldering flames sprouting from their mouths. Instead, before her lay an empty hall bereft of carpet and pillar and brazier. The passage was dark, with a solitary string light hanging here and there from the ceiling to guide those making their way from one end of the room to the other. In the dim lighting, Ginger could just make out a pointed throne patched together with cardboard and matches, as well as a mouse that sat upon it. It was only when she drew nearer that she could perceive the creature's appearance: his fur was red, nearly auburn in tone; most of his body was draped not in a regal robe but in leather armor, material that had apparently been pulled from a human's old boot and shaped to fit a mouse. His head was quite noticeably crownless, his eyes were golden-brown, his whiskers were glossy, his tail was as long as his body and coiled around him, and both his paws were palms-down on the handle of a sharp paring knife. Ginger shuddered. Even if the mouse did not plan to use that weapon on her (which was yet to be determined), the idea that he was strong enough to wield it was terrifying.

Ginger had difficulty remembering court etiquette, but she figured it would be best to kneel and wait until she was verbally summoned. Now bending the legs in any manner is no easy task for a gingerbread woman, so in her attempt to do so, Ginger toppled over and fell flat on her face. It was embarrassing, but perhaps the regent would see her act as a show of meaningful homage. Indeed, she had heard tales of people prostrating themselves before their betters.

"What in Great Boris's whiskers are you doing on the floor?" asked the mouse. "Get up, will you?"

Ginger remained facedown; perhaps this was a test. "I—I wanted to show you the respect you deserve, O king."

"King?" She could hear the mouse rise. "I'm no king, and I deserve no such reverence. Stand, please. I'm getting uncomfortable."

With great caution, she pushed herself into a standing position. The mouse was upright and between her and the throne, his knife now strapped to his back and his earnest eyes staring at her. "Not a king?" she muttered. "That— that's a major plot twist. I think I'm going to need a minute."

"Take all the time you need."

She swung her arm toward him. "Okay, riddle me this! If you aren't a king, then why do you have a throne?"

"They insisted on building it for me," he answered. "What am I going to do, not sit on it? Can you imagine the rudeness?" He sighed. "Anyway, even in this darkness I'm sure you can see that no crown sits on my head. And what did you think—that I ruled a kingdom of fifteen mice?"

She tapped the ends of her arms together awkwardly. "I didn't want to assume anything."

"That's wise," he pointed out. He began to pace with his hands behind his back, but he drew no closer to her. "The truth is that I am on the run currently, being pursued by an enemy, and this 'kingdom' that you see around me is no more than a bivouac. We will need to be on the move before long."

Ginger pressed both hands to her face in shock. "You're being pursued? By whom?"

The mouse allowed a lengthy pause to hang in the air before he stopped pacing and turned to her. "With all due respect, miss, that does not concern you—especially since we have not yet been formerly introduced." He crossed several inches of hallway and extended a hand to her with an apprehensive smile. "I am called Klaus."

"Ginger," she replied, taking his hand and bowing her head briefly. "And how cute! Your name rhymes with 'mouse.'"

Klaus coughed. "Purely coincidental, I'm sure." He released her arm but continued to smile. "Now I must ask: what brings a living gingerbread cookie—one that bears an unusual aroma of rosemary, I might add—to my doorstep on Christmas Eve?"

Ginger frowned. *Rosemary. A painful reminder.* "I didn't intend to intrude, Mr. Klaus. I had no idea that fine mice such as yourselves were back here. It's just...I'm looking for my brother. Molasses is his name. I thought that he might have been hiding in the space behind the cabinets, but clearly I was mistaken."

He scrunched his mouth and clasped his hands together in thought. "Molasses—a cookie like yourself? I may have some information for you. One similar to you, and with the same scent, was spotted in this very house not an hour ago. But I'm going to need you to do something for me before I give you that information."

Oh no! thought Ginger, *I'm going to become a five-course meal, I just know it! Look at him! He's all lithe and wiry and could use a cookie or two!* Instead, she just said, "Name it. Whatever I need to do to find my brother."

"I need you to tell me your story," he said, turning from her and sitting again on his throne. "My allies and I have seen many cookies in our time, but none that could speak or move. Not until tonight. So tell me: how did you and your brother come to be? And why have you two been separated?"

Ginger stood there a moment, weighing her options. She could tell Klaus the truth; he seemed a nice enough fellow. Then again, looks could be deceiving, and it was possible that Molasses had already been among this ragtag group and recruited them to his cause. If she were to lie, however—well, something made her think that Klaus was wise and discerning, and that he would see right through her. She felt she had no choice but to give him the benefit of the doubt and share all that had happened, all that she had been trying to suppress.

Thus, she regaled him with the tale of Mr. Theo and his annual cookie delivery, and of the love that man possessed for both the townspeople and his craft. She told him of the baker's latest batch of gingerbread cookies, and how a portion of the batter had been quickened by the man's affections. She recalled the first moments of her consciousness, when she had found that she could both hear and speak, and how she had soon thereafter gazed upon the face of her maker. As she unfurled the tale, Klaus listened with great respect and attentiveness, his head cupped in his paws. He dared not interject until the story had been told in full.

"Molasses and I noticed that a man was watching from the other side of the house after Mr. Theo had started speaking to us," she said. "I later found out that was Mr. Theo's son, Tanas, a man who has spent most of his life envying his father. You see, Mr. Theo has long pleased the people of Sprinkleton with his cookies, using the same perfect recipes all these years; there was no need to alter his ingredients, nor would it be in his character to do so. But Tanas, who some years ago decided to take up the family business, thought he could surpass his father. He wanted to make *better* cookies, and he craved fame and fortune, so he dishonored his father not only by refusing to stick to the original recipes, but also by adding ingredients to those recipes—ingredients that clashed with the originals. He opened his own shop and peddled his wares to the villagers.

"Sadly, some people enjoyed his twisted creations, but most saw his wares for what they were: corrupted knockoffs of the true, pure cookies that his father had always made. And some laughed and scoffed at him, telling him that he was unable to come up with his own recipe, but could only taint a good recipe that had long existed. So Tanas's envy toward his father grew, and grew...and that night, when he saw that Mr. Theo had managed to bring some of his cookies *to life*, that was the final straw.

"After Molasses and I jumped up from the cookie sheet, Mr. Theo showed us great kindness by giving us faces and clothes with the frosting from his kitchen; then he stayed up with us late into the night, speaking to us and making us feel most welcome. Every night afterwards, when he had finished working at the bakery or spending time at community events, he returned home and spoke to us. During the day, Molasses and I would take care of the house and get to know each other better. I learned that my brother was enamored by Mr. Theo's house and his creations, and that he loved our creator as much as I did. When we were not working, we would race each other across the living room or fling spoonfuls of frosting at each other or see who could climb the tallest piece of furniture. Molasses usually won in any tests of strength or speed, but we had so much fun together!

"One day, while Mr. Theo was in the back yard, Tanas crept into the house and introduced himself. He came across to us as very likeable and ambitious, and he had this infectious energy that we both admired. After he had gained our trust, he told us that we were incomplete, that we were just shadows of what we *could* be, and that he could give us anything we desired. He said that Mr. Theo had never intended for this to be our final form, and that we were meant for something more—but only he had the skill to change us. Molasses was thrilled, and although I was skeptical, I couldn't help but wonder if maybe I had been slighted somehow. You know, maybe there was more to life than what Mr. Theo had shown us. Maybe there was a whole world out there that he had held us back from seeing! So we agreed to be changed, not yet knowing the evil that was in Tanas's heart.

"Somehow, he did change us. I don't know how. I'm not sure if he threw together his own awful mix of spices, added that to our finished forms, and then stuck us back in the oven....That would make the most sense to me. But when we awoke in a tray on the counter, something was very different. Molasses was no longer the same; *I* was no longer the same. It seemed like we knew more than we had before, and there was this new...sense of independence. Whatever Tanas did altered us on the inside, but we looked the same on the outside.

"The change in Molasses was much more obvious. He became short-tempered, violent, and angry. He also seemed happy about the change and kept pouring out gratitude to Tanas. Of course, the man tried to show humility and shrug aside all the praise, but I thought it was clear that he was basking in it. I felt sick somehow, but I didn't want to appear ungrateful; I thanked him for empowering us. I think he then became convinced that we would do anything for him as repayment for what he had done for us. That turned out to be half-true...and that—that was when we were given our orders."

Klaus leaned forward, waiting for her to continue. When she did not, he asked, "What orders were given?"

Ginger trembled at the thought, but no tears came to her eyes. She was fairly sure she was physically unable to cry. "Tanas cursed his father's work. He thought that the citizens of Sprinkleton were idiots for accepting Mr. Theo's cookies without question. He claimed that their palates were unrefined, and that they didn't deserve to enjoy cookies of any kind! So he told us that every batch of Mr. Theo's cookies in town must be changed the same way we had been changed. 'If the Sprinkletonians aren't going to enjoy my cookies,' he said, 'then they shouldn't enjoy any cookies ever again.' It was only then that I realized we had been poisoned. Not that we ingested poison, but rather, if we were eaten, we could cause harm to others!

"Molasses left, perfectly willing to do Tanas's bidding. I told the man that I would do the very same, but in truth, I dashed into the back yard and told Mr. Theo everything. It brought him sorrow, I knew, but it almost seemed as though he had been expecting his son to take such drastic measures after all those years of envy. He told me that his son's corruption was now obvious in me—and not just the rosemary smell, which seems to be a signature ingredient of his son's. He said he had the means of relieving me of the new foreign ingredients, but it would take time, possibly even years. I have to confess—and maybe it's just a result of what Tanas did to me and my brother—but I found myself doubting Mr. Theo's abilities. How could he cure us of something that ran so deep? I could feel the depth of the change within me, and it seemed so...impossible for anyone, even the world's greatest baker, to undo what had happened.

"But then he gave me orders of his own: to find my brother, stop him from poisoning the cookies throughout Sprinkleton, and bring him home. I vowed to do so, and he took me outside and showed me the town from his house on the hill. Some might find Sprinkleton tiny, but for a lone cookie like me, it might as well have been its own planet! I felt intimidated but mentioned that I would head to the nearest home at the foot of the hill. And so I was off, nearly an hour behind my brother when I left...and I haven't seen a sign of him since I've been here." She brought her arms together, an imploring gesture. "And that's it; now you know everything. So I have to ask: please, sir, if you really do have news of my brother's whereabouts, you *must* tell me. Please! I can't bear the thought of all those people getting sick, or worse, because of our mistakes."

Klaus rose from his throne again, his face contorted in deep thought. He took a few steps to the left, his tail slithering on the ground behind him; he took a few steps to the right, his whiskers bristling from the movement. The string lights reflected off the paring knife that hung at his back, and his leather armor squeaked as he walked. "Your brother was in this house," he said at length. "He was very stealthy, but we spotted him. We didn't attack him because we were unaware of his intentions, but his acts were...odd. After one of our watchmen saw him and alerted us, we watched as your brother climbed onto the kitchen island— with the lights on and the family chatting nearby!—and lifted the lid of the cookie tin, tearing the sticker on its edge in the process. Then he jumped inside and was there for less than a minute before he came back out, removed the old sticker, and replaced it with a fresh one that had been sitting in a satchel around his waist."

Ginger thought she could feel her eyes grow wide. "Are you telling me that Molasses has already poisoned this family's cookies?"

"I'm telling you that I believe your tale," answered Klaus. "I'm telling you that I find your brother to be a danger to the humans of this town, and therefore a danger to all of mousedom."

Ginger gasped. "It's true! But tell me, sir, what can I do now that he has the advantage and is so far ahead?"

"One way or another, he must be stopped." Klaus drew his sword and held it in both hands. "I told you that I'm not a king, but I may be, some day. What kind of leader would I be if I let this threat go unchecked?"

"You're going after Molasses on your own?" cried Ginger.

"No, not on my own. I'll have you with me, won't I?" Klaus winked at her and made for the wood slat on the other side of the hall. "Come on! Don't linger; we are already running behind. It's time for us to save Christmas."

CHAPTER 3
Not Even a Klaus

  To say Ginger was elated to have a new travel buddy would be an understatement. Not only did she have the companionship of a mouse, but on her side was a *leader* of mice, and one who could wear leather armor and wield a kitchen knife like a claymore. He also seemed both friendly and honorable, which was a major plus; no one liked to be accompanied by a grumpy goose with a shady disposition, after all. It did not hurt that mice were known to have an amazing sense of smell, as well. With her brother reeking of the same rosemary extract that tainted her, surely they would find him in no time.

  After they had said their farewells to the Colony Behind the Cabinets (there were more than a few tears shed, and their leader was obliged to share some encouraging words with several of the mice in turn), Ginger and Klaus were off into the dark, Klaus leading the way. When they had reached the cabinet by which Ginger had first entered the recess, he told her to take hold of his tail. She did so, and before she could ask why she was doing such a thing, he suddenly scrambled up the back of the cabinet with her in tow. To her shame she nearly screamed, not only because she feared she might fall, but also because the paring knife on Klaus's back threatened to make her half the cookie she used to be. Fortunately, he was able to bear her and avoid causing her harm, and the next thing she knew, they were sitting on the floor inside the cabinet. Klaus was clearly doing his best not to breathe too hard after such an exercise, but she knew the truth: although immensely beautiful, she was not the lightest cookie. She would have gone on a diet days ago, but cookies actually do not eat, so there was nothing to be done.

Klaus tiptoed to the cabinet door and opened it in utter silence. Ginger strafed over to him and peeked out into the kitchen. Thankfully, not a creature was stirring in the vicinity, and the sounds of the humans snoring could be heard in the distance. The cookie tin still rested on the counter, untouched—as far as Ginger could tell—since she had beheld it several minutes ago. She also noticed that over to the left, the cookies that the family had left for Santa were uneaten. She shook her head in disappointment. The ruddy gift-giver was really slacking tonight.

She nudged Klaus as he scanned the area. "What's the plan?" she asked him. "Any sign of Molasses?"

Klaus frowned. "After your brother poisoned the cookies, he jumped from the kitchen island to the counter and slipped out the window. Why these people leave their window open a crack during the cold of winter is beyond me. But yes, Molasses's scent leads out that window." His eyes moved up to the cookie tin. "As for our plan, the family keeps a trash can on the opposite side of the kitchen island. One of us needs to hold down the lever of the trash can to keep it ajar; the other needs to open the lid of the cookies and push the tin off the edge of the counter into the trash. No human in his right mind would eat a cookie covered in congealed cooking oil and wet coffee grounds."

"You assume these humans are in their right minds," Ginger pointed out.

"True. It's a gamble, but one that we must make."

Ginger sighed. "Obviously, I—the whale of our merry duo—will hold down the lever. You use your super-mouse strength to push the cookie tin. Are we agreed?"

Klaus nodded. "Agreed."

"Great!" She clapped her arms together. "One last thing: after the cookies crash into the can with a loud racket, how are we going to escape before the family can investigate?"

"The same way we climbed up the back of that cabinet just now," the mouse told her. "I'll jump down from the countertop, and we'll run over to the cabinets by the kitchen window. You hang on to my tail, I'll scale the cabinet door, and we'll slip out the open window unseen."

"Do you really think we'll have time to do all of that?"

"We better. I don't think humans would take kindly to a living cookie and a mouse wielding a knife."

If Ginger had possessed teeth, she would have gritted them. "Is this the best plan we have?"

"Unless you have one, it's the *only* plan we have," said Klaus. He let a few seconds of silence hang in the air in case she had something to offer. Then with a stern look he asked, "Are you ready?"

"Definitely not," she answered, "but let's get on with it."

Although more than a bit dubious, Ginger managed to develop a single-mindedness about and wholehearted devotion to their plan. That was why she was so caught off guard by what happened next. As she and Klaus were dashing across the cold kitchen floor, something flew by in her peripheral vision. She stopped in her tracks and gazed across the living room to find an unusual sight: a cookie, shaped like a reindeer, was prancing through the air outside the window looking out into the front yard. Stranger still was the fact that he carried a scroll in his mouth. As soon as he had caught sight of Ginger, he engaged in a celebratory midair dance and motioned toward the front door. She exchanged a wary glance with Klaus, and when she had turned her focus back to the window, the reindeer cookie was gone. But she could hear paper slipping beneath the front door off to the left, followed by a couple of light knocks; she guessed that was intended to relay the message, "Read it."

"A trap?" she asked Klaus.

"Could be," he said with a shrug. "Only one way to find out."

They crossed the carpet, and once they had reached the door, Klaus began to open the scroll while Ginger kept watch. He pocketed the small ribbon that had kept the scroll intact and opened the page. The room was still illuminated only by Christmas lights, but she could tell that the words on the document had been penned by none other than her maker. His script was humble but elegant, and in it was a sort of commanding quality that arrested the attention.

Klaus cleared his throat and read aloud:

My dearest Ginger,

I hope that this letter finds you well. As I am sure you have now seen for yourself, you and Molasses are not the only cookies that have been given life. Shortly after you left, I took my latest batches of cookies out of the oven, and every one of them rose from the pan! Some of them remained by my side, such as the faithful reindeer that delivered this message to you. But others ran off in different directions, the scent of rosemary lingering in their wake. So you see, my dear girl...the situation has become much more dire than ever before. The cookies came freshly from the oven and were not given the same malicious commission that was bestowed upon Molasses; but should you encounter these corrupted creations during your journey, do not be surprised if they seek to stop you from rescuing your brother. If they keep you from completing your task, the Sprinkletonians may not make it through Christmas alive.

Be cautious, Ginger. Be watchful. And remember: redemption is promised to those willing to reject the corruption within.

Come home to me.

Most sincerely yours,

"I didn't know mice could read," whispered Ginger.

"I didn't know cookies could walk," Klaus retorted.

"That's fair." She stared at the letter in the mouse's hand. "This is terrible news. It seemed hard enough to find my brother out here in this large town and stop him from harming everyone. Now he has...allies."

"Many allies, it sounds like," said Klaus thoughtfully. "And according to Mr. Theo, although they haven't been commanded to poison Sprinkleton's cookies, they may be inclined to oppose our mission."

"The two of us may not be enough," said Ginger, feeling a sense of hopelessness wash over her. "Can we ask your mouse colony to help us with this?"

"They need to remain where they are for reasons I can't go into right now; it's for their safety. I told them before I left that if I had not returned within two hours of sunrise, they should head out into town. But we can't spare the time to tell them the situation has changed. We need to hold to our current task and rely on subterfuge as much as possible."

She placed both arms on the side of her head. "I don't know. I don't think I can do this, Klaus."

"Yes, you can," he told her gently. "Your gracious creator has entrusted you with this honorable duty. That's all you need to know." He rolled up the scroll and put it in his pocket. "Let's focus on one thing at a time: our task is to dump the poisoned cookies into the trash. Once we have accomplished that, we can move on to other matters."

Ginger nodded at him hesitantly. "Yes, you're— you're right. At the very least, we need to do that." She did her best to shake away the fear. "Okay, back to the kitchen we go!"

They raced across the carpet and, without a word to each other, went to their respective positions. Klaus clawed his way up the side of the kitchen island, and Ginger hurried over to the trash can. She saw that there was a lever at the base of the can that was used to open the lid, as Klaus had described. Half a second later she could hear the cookie tin moving across the countertop, inch by inch, a quiet screech ringing out with its every movement. She took a deep breath and swung her arms in front of her once, twice, three times. Then, with all the athleticism she could muster, she leapt up onto the lever.

"This thing," said Klaus, out of breath, "this thing is way heavier than it looks. Just how many cookies does Mr. Theo give to each family?"

"At least three dozen," she responded.
"But...um...Klaus? I seem to have a problem of my own."

"What is it?"

"Well, apparently, I'm not heavy enough to weigh down the lever." It was a happy problem, to be certain. She would have to boast to Molasses later, if there *was* a later. "We're going to need something else to weigh it down."

Klaus had just managed to get the cookie tin right to the edge of the counter, overlooking the trash can. He seemed spent by the exercise. "I—I'm going to need you to figure that one out, Ginger. Find something heavy that wouldn't look too out of place being on the floor of a kitchen—anything!"

She looked here and there, but the kitchen was hauntingly immaculate; the owners of the house left little in plain sight. There was a broom over by the fridge that was much too long for her to carry, a stepstool thrice her height and ten times her width, and Christmas presents under the tree that had no business being anywhere else. Then she remembered that when she had peered into one of the cabinets earlier, she had seen a bag of potatoes—big, whopping Russet potatoes. *That could work*, she told herself, seeing a glimmer of hope. *Please work.*

When she had managed to heave one of the huge spuds out of the cabinet, Klaus palmed his face. "A potato isn't going to be heavy enough!"

She tried to roll her eyes at him, forgetting her absence of irises. "Don't you know about momentum, Klaus?"

"Not really!"

"You mean you know how to read, but you don't know about momentum?"

"Never heard of it!" He wiped some sweat from his brow. "Whatever you're going to do, you need to do it quickly!"

"Okay, but your timing needs to be impeccable. I might only be able to get the trash can open for a second."

"That's fine!"

She feared that it *wasn't* fine, but now wasn't the time for doubt. With many a grunt, she tugged the potato across the floor and over to the base of the large can. Then, bending her knees as much as was physically possible, she hoisted the vegetable onto the lever. It did not open the lid fully, as she suspected, but it was up nearly halfway; and besides, she had thought of a contingency plan.

"Now, Ginger!" Klaus called out to her. "Let's go!"

She climbed onto the spud and stood up straight. "Get ready!" she shouted. Then she leapt high into the air and brought all her weight down upon the potato. The force of her heavy cookie-body hitting the tuber caused the lever to go down and the lid to go up. Klaus, with greater alacrity than she could believe, shoved the cookie tin off the edge of the counter that very instant. She was happy to see that he had popped the lid off the tin first; as it plunged down toward the trash can, it flipped upside down and its lid was thrown to the side. The cookies went into the trash bag, but both the tin and its lid clanged *extremely* loudly against the floor. Ginger watched with dread as the lid spun against the tile. She also noticed, amidst the chaos, that the label Molasses had replaced was *similar* to the one Mr. Theo used but was not the *same*; Mr. Theo's sticker had a white background and a red reindeer rearing up with its legs to the left, whereas *this* sticker had a grey background and a red reindeer rearing up with its legs to the right. *A cheap knockoff,* she thought, *just like the cookies that Tanas makes.*

"What the smell was that?" asked a man's voice, most likely from a nearby bedroom.

"We need to go, Ginger!" Klaus demanded, and it was only then that she realized he was already on the ground beside her. "Come on! Up the counter and out the window. There's no time to lose!"

He led the way toward the kitchen sink, and she stopped but a moment so she could seize the potato and toss it as closely as she could to the cabinet from which it had been removed. Klaus leapt onto the slick wood door, and she jumped up after him and pressed both of her arms against his tail. He scurried his way up, up, up...but something was wrong.

"Johnny, look at this!" cried a female voice in the hallway just beyond the kitchen. "Did you leave the cookies on the edge of the counter? You did this last year!"

Klaus was making decent headway up the cabinet, but he was straining and slipping every couple of inches. It was not her weight alone that was hindering him, Ginger knew. He had put everything he had into pushing that tin of cookies across the counter, and it had very possibly weighed over a pound, something that even five mice together would have had trouble with. It was a miracle that he had been able to move it at all, and he had moved it well over four feet.

"I'm not going to make it," he told her. "I need you to climb up my back and jump to the top of the counter."

"What?" she cried. "I'm not—"

"Do it, now!" he told her.

She listened to him. Scrambling up his back and avoiding his knife, she reached the back of his head and propelled herself upward at the same moment that he released his grip on the cabinet door. She saw him plunge down toward the kitchen floor, but she did not see him hit it, as she had just made it over the lip of the counter and onto the edge of the sink. As she pushed herself into a standing position, she heard a gasp.

"A mouse, Johnny!" the woman exclaimed. "A mouse on Christmas Eve! Get the traps!"

Be safe, Klaus, Ginger said to herself with immense sorrow. Knowing that she could not risk the split second it would take to look back, she skirted the edge of the sink, leapt onto the windowsill, and slipped out of the house and into the night.

CHAPTER 4
Sprinkleton Scuffle

Melancholy was not the only feeling that settled on Ginger as she alighted upon the earth; there was also a sense of awe, triggered by the view of multicolored lights framing the roof of every home, the sounds of looping Christmas music playing in some yards, and the thin layer of snow upon the ground. The image was nothing new, as she had beheld the very same from Mr. Theo's house on the hill since she had been created, but it never failed to mesmerize her. If only Klaus were there beside her to enjoy the yuletide vista; after all, she had observed in the Colony Behind the Cabinets that they kept Christmas in their own way. Perhaps all of nature, from the miniscule mouse to the roaring river to the majestic mountain, somehow surmised the significance of the season and celebrated it in a million unique voices.

She did not know how long to wait there, considering, hoping, grieving. *Just how long is appropriate to wait for someone who sacrificed himself to save his friend?* Ginger wondered. *Klaus was exhausted, and one of the humans spotted him. Did he really have enough energy to run away from them?* Every few seconds she looked up at the window, but she saw neither fur nor whisker for what seemed like an eternity. When at last one of the humans slammed the window shut, she slumped over and concluded that Klaus, whatever his fate, would not be rejoining her. It was a disheartening conclusion, but also the very thing she needed to spur her on. *He wanted us to hurry,* she remembered. *He knew the stakes and was trying to get us out of the house as quickly as possible. To wait too long out here and risk the poisoning of cookies by Molasses would only dishonor Klaus.* She looked ahead at the nearest house. *I no longer have his strong nose to help me, but it's most likely that Molasses would have gone straight out the window and to that house right there. Then that's it; nothing more to think about. Time to get back to it, Ginger.*

Between her and the next house was a hill covered with bark and frost, which she scaled with some difficulty. A single string of white Christmas lights loomed overhead, extending from the house she had left to a shrub that was perched on the peak of the hill. As she ascended ever higher, she cast an occasional glance to her left at the small but sprawling town, and again she felt the overwhelming sense that her task was insurmountable. It took ten of her footsteps to travel the distance of one human footstep, and her brother was both faster and well ahead of her; it was even possible that she was aiming for the wrong house! Ginger struggled to grasp her maker's wisdom. Could he not have taken his motorized bike, gone door-to-door, and warned each household of the danger to come? Did he care so little for his peers that, instead of owning up to his mistakes, he had sent a living cookie to do his dirty work? Or was there more going on that Ginger in her limited knowledge was unaware of? While she wrestled with her doubts, she suddenly gazed through the darkness and saw Mr. Theo's modest house resting on the hill, its circular white Christmas lights gleaming brightly, and a warm glow emanating from its front door. She let out a sigh and thought, *I don't understand everything; all I can do is lean on his goodness and kindness to me and do what he has asked.*

She was rather proud of herself when she had finally managed to clamber to the top of the hill, but there was no time to celebrate. Before her was a scene she could not have imagined in her wildest dreams: Molasses and two cookies were standing on a windowsill of the home just a few feet away, exerting all their effort to pry up the window; amassed near them was a small army of Christmas cookies—

gingerbread men and women, snowmen, and Christmas trees. The cookies were turned toward the window, watching (those who had eyes, anyway) with excited expectation. Ginger was far too frightened to count the number of her enemies, but even a cursory look told her that there were nearly thirty. She froze in place and considered her next move. It would be unwise to run with reckless abandon toward her brother and decry his deeds, unproductive to try to blend in with those around her, and self-destructive to start attacking the minions of Tanas. What other choice did she have?

Subterfuge, she remembered Klaus telling her, although now that she thought about it, how did the mouse know about subterfuge and not about momentum? She decided that the best course of action, presently, was to hide behind the shrub that stood at the top of the hill, collect herself, try to enter the house from a different direction, and confront her brother alone once he got inside. She swung one leg over and faced the shrub, around which the string of white Christmas lights had been wound tightly. Just as she was about to take a step forward, she heard a voice call out to her, loud and strong, disrupting the otherwise silent night: "Ginger!"

She turned back around slowly, hoping that by delaying her turn she might delay the inevitable conflict. To her horror, the many cookies were now facing her, including Molasses. He and the two gingerbread men on the windowsill had propped open the window just enough so that he would be able to squeeze his way inside. He was standing there, his beady black eyes studying her. In most ways he looked the same: he was much like her in appearance but with frosting pants and a frosting shirt instead of a dress; he also wore a dark green bowtie rather than a bow on his head. In fact, when he had departed from Mr. Theo's house earlier in the evening, his head had been bare—but now he wore what seemed to be a sort of pirate hat fashioned from a bit of red and green giftwrap. Two satchels were slung across his chest, one—Ginger assumed—

carrying Tanas's ingredients and the other holding the knockoff cookie tin labels.

"Ginger, isn't this a fine evening?" he asked her. "I managed to take care of my first house pretty quickly, but I'm hoping to pick up the pace on this next one. And look! I just finished explaining our mission to our kin here, and they've agreed to help us. Isn't that great? We'll be finished in no time!"

She did not know what to say; she was paralyzed with dread, and the only thing that was clear to her was that she could not say anything to affirm that what her brother was doing was right and good. All she could do was scan the cookies between her and Molasses and feel regret that she had not arrived sooner. The conscience of these cookies had already been darkened by Tanas's ingredients, and now her brother had deepened that darkness.

"How is your progress, Ginger?" her brother inquired, though there was something in his voice that implied he doubted her devotion to the cause.

"I—I have no progress," she replied sheepishly.

Some of the cookies chuckled and others sneered, but Molasses appeared unmoved by her response. "That's okay," he said. "Not all of us can be strong or fast, and the night is young still. Here! Come up here and we can tackle this next house together."

Part of her—the part that had been tainted by Tanas's recipe, she understood—wanted to move forward and accept his offer. It would be more comfortable and far less dangerous, and her life would be spared, and she could enjoy a reunion with her brother; and yet something deeper inside told her that the easiest path was not always the best one, and that immediate comfort and a lack of peril could eventually lead to an utter lack of the former and an all-enveloping presence of the latter. She also thought of the townspeople who would suffer if she failed to speak up. And so she looked away from the cookies directly before her and met her brother's gaze, and a courage filled her, a courage that seemed alien to her—one that she would never be able to explain. She could not remain silent.

"I haven't come to help you, Molasses," she told him, hearing a surprising strength in her voice. "I've come to stop you."

There was a small gasp among several of the cookies, as well as a few scoffs and snickers. Molasses said nothing for several seconds, but he did not seem all that surprised. He simply shook his head and let out a long sigh. "Oh, Ginger, Ginger. Before I left you at Mr. Theo's house, Tanas called me back to him and shared that he did not believe you would seek to fulfill his commission. He thought that you lied to him, and that you would try to thwart us. I didn't want to believe it, but I see now that he was right."

She felt even greater courage surging into her. "Tanas was able to recognize deceit because he, himself, is a deceiver. He has deceived you, Molasses, and through you all our kin who stand here!"

There was much grumbling among the cookies, but three or four at least appeared to consider her statement. They seemed eager to hear more, so she spoke up again.

"This is not the way we should be behaving!" she declared. "Should cookies cause harm to others? Should it please us to bring pain? No! That is not what we were meant to do! We were meant to bring joy! By fulfilling Tanas's plan, we are going against the very standard that our maker set for us. It's unnatural!"

"It doesn't *feel* unnatural," Molasses pointed out. "It feels right. What we're doing is what we feel we ought to do."

Her voice fell, not because of a lack of confidence but because of sorrow. "It doesn't matter what we *feel* is right; it matters what *is* right. That's not up to us to decide."

Molasses hesitated and looked here and there at the cookies who hung on his every word. His head dropped, as in mourning, and he turned away from her and back to the window. "If only you were more like us, Sister. If only you could see the foolishness of your thinking. Unfortunately, I don't have the time to debate with you; I have a mission I need to complete."

"Molasses, don't you go in there!" she shouted.

"There's nothing you can do to stop me. But if you're intent on getting in our way, we *will* stop you." He turned to the cookie on his right. "Get rid of her, but please make it quick. For my sake."

The gingerbread man nodded at him, and Molasses dipped under the opening in the window. His ally took a step forward on the windowsill and stretched his arm toward Ginger. "The impostor is an enemy of our father, and therefore an enemy of us all. She mustn't be allowed to live! Cookies of Tanas, attack!"

Ginger was in disbelief that her own brother would allow such a travesty to take place, and she half-expected him to show up at the window again and call off the attack. But he was gone, his evil scheme consuming his every thought, and he was very likely spreading the poison that would claim lives. She knew she could not outrun the host before her, so she closed her eyes, threw her arms in front of her face, and hoped for a merciful end. She peeked a moment later, and with distress she could tell that the horde would be on her any second. *I did the best I could*, she thought, and she wondered if her maker could hear her. *I gave it everything I had, but my brother is too far gone. He won't see reason. And now I have no choice but to give up.* She caught a glance of Mr. Theo's house on the hill. *Thank you for everything, Mr. Theo.*

An unusual sound came from behind her, and whatever it was caused some of the cookies—four of whom were just a few inches away—to falter. She turned around and beheld a most astonishing sight: Klaus, using the ribbon from Mr. Theo's letter that he had pocketed earlier, was sliding down the string of Christmas lights that reached from the house to the nearby shrub. As he drew nearer, he let out a mighty war cry and then released the ribbon with one hand; he pulled a chunk of cheese from his pocket with his free hand, took a bite, and then released the ribbon altogether. The moment he landed beside Ginger, he seized his paring knife from his back and brandished it with a wide slash, chopping the four enemies around her in pieces. His act had saved Ginger's life, yet she saw that it was only a moment's reprieve. Still the army of cookies came on, undaunted, making their relentless approach like two dozen mindless zombies. They never could have anticipated fifteen more mice appearing as if from thin air, racing over the crest of the hill, past Ginger, and directly into their battle lines.

Klaus led the charge, wielding his knife as a human would a broadsword, his every strike true, and his fearlessness palpable. On his flank were Horace and Arthur; Horace swung his dried cherry stem around and knocked the cookies onto their backs, while Arthur, being quite the substantial brute of a mouse, wrecked his opponents to the side with his sheer size and speed. Ingrid followed close behind, flinging rubber bands with a strength that belied her size, and many of the adversarial cookies lost a leg or a trunk at the mercy of her accuracy. The eleven other mice fanned out, an assortment of weapons at their disposal: some lobbed pebbles with slings made of cloth, some charged with toothpicks held out in front of them like spears, and some used cardboard shields to knock the cookies off balance.

Ginger watched the display before her, too stunned to move. She was not inclined to join the fray, not because she believed it was wrong to fight against evil at times, but because her mind was still on Molasses—*and* because the mice seemed to have everything well in hand. Although the rodents were outnumbered nearly two-to-one, their skill and obvious experience made them more than a match for their enemies. Many cookies fell before their onslaught in a matter of seconds, while some surrendered almost immediately. There was a group of less than ten, however—which included the two gingerbread who had assisted Molasses with the window—who refused to either fall or yield. This group resisted with great skill, dodging the strikes of the rodents and knocking several of them unconscious. When eventually they perceived that the battle was against them, one among them called for a tactical retreat, and the others listened; they fled in every direction, and the mice began to go after them. But Klaus, clearly concerned about spreading his forces too thin, gave the order for his allies not to give chase. They heeded his command and remained on the battlefield, where they tended to their wounded and confronted their prisoners.

It was strange how everything had changed in less than two minutes; but there Ginger stood, her persecutors either slain or turned or gone, while she had managed to stand where she was, unscathed. The conclusion of the battle broke her free of her stasis, and she stepped forward as Klaus walked toward her. She was pleased to see that, although a few cookie crumbs mottled his fur, he was unhurt. He returned his paring knife to his back and inclined his head toward her.

"Klaus," she said, leaping forward and hugging him, "I thought that I had lost you."

"You almost did," he admitted.

"What happened?"

He took a deep breath, as if reliving the moment was less than desirable. "Well, I assumed that my life was forfeit when the humans spotted me—that I would either stumble my way into a trap or be smashed with a boot. I ran as fast as I could and had just enough strength to crawl back into the cabinet leading to our bivouac. But I was too weary to climb the cord leading into the space behind the cabinets."

Ginger released him and threw her arms to her face. "What did you do?"

"I did nothing. I closed my eyes and waited for the end, but it didn't come. Instead, I opened my eyes again and saw that the Colony—my friends—were all around me." Ginger could swear that tears were creeping into his eyes. "Even though I had sternly warned them not to leave our shelter, their loyalty outweighed their fear, and they had agreed amongst one another that they would go after us. I—I suppose they somehow assessed the seriousness of the situation."

She did not think she could be any more amazed. "But how did you recover your strength so quickly and get out of the house?"

He smiled at her. "We mice love cheese, my dear Ginger. My friends had taken along several small blocks and handed me one right away. A few bites were all I needed to give me the energy to lead us out of the house." He laughed. "If only I had thought of taking along some cheese myself! And to answer the second part of your question, we mice can fit through the tiniest of holes, and even the most carefully constructed buildings have a crevice or two. We found a way out through the attic, and as soon as we were on the roof, we could see your predicament. I asked my allies to make a ground assault while I came in from above...and you know the rest."

"Thank you, my friend," she told him. "Thank you for not giving up on our quest, even though you had already done more than enough. Thank you for saving me." Because she could not cry, she did her best to relay her gratitude through her voice. "And please extend my thanks to all the mice of your colony."

"Of course," he replied, inclining his head again. "But as much as I enjoy chatting with a delightful cookie such as yourself, we have an urgent matter to attend to, don't we?"

Ginger nodded. "Molasses."

"Indeed." He turned away from her and looked upon the battlefield and his companions. The few mice who had been unconscious were now standing; some of them were using strands of tree bark or plant fibers to bind the hands of their captives, and others were discussing the glories of battle. "And yet Molasses is not the only threat. We will go to him in a moment, together; allow me to first address the Colony."

She pressed her arms together. "Please do."

Klaus cleared his throat, garnering the attention of both the mice and the freshly bound cookies. He lifted his voice so that all in the area could hear him: "My brethren, you have fought well this day. It's an honor to lead you, and indeed, I don't feel worthy of being considered a king in your eyes. You have shown such kindness to me and to my friend Ginger."

"Any friend of yours is a friend of ours!" Horace called out, waving his cherry-stem cane. An array of voices followed, chanting their agreement.

"And that's something we're both grateful for," Klaus said, putting a hand on Ginger's back. "You have sacrificed much by leaving our shelter; we know the risk of being exposed while our pursuer seeks our lives. And so it pains me to ask more of you."

"Ask it!" yelled Arthur. More assents came from the mice around him.

Klaus smiled at their willingness to serve. "The Cookies of Tanas have fled, and we don't know what kind of harm, if any, they'll do out of spite over their defeat. Perhaps they'll try to carry out the mission of their friend Molasses." He waved a hand toward the group. "Providentially, there are fifteen of you here and, as we know, fifteen homes throughout Sprinkleton. Once you have tucked our captives away in our hideout, I think that for the safety of our town, it would be wise for us to spread out and walk the perimeter of each house until daybreak; that way, any of the surviving corrupted cookies will be unlikely to enter."

"A fine plan!" Ingrid chimed in, smiling. "Fifteen mice and fifteen homes. A mouse for every house!"

"A mouse for every house." Klaus grinned. "Well said, Ingrid. And may I just say that your fur is positively radiant tonight?"

Ginger was not certain, but she thought she saw the female mouse blush. "That's very kind of my king to say, though he looks handsomer than ever, handsomer than Great Boris himself."

The two stared at each other across the battleground, leaving Ginger with a deep feeling of discomfort. When at last it became unbearable, she nudged her friend. "Um...Klaus?"

"Oh, yes, onward," he said, turning his head toward her. "Anything you'd like to add before we go?"

Ginger gazed at those who had risked everything to save her life. She did not like public speaking, but she figured that these mice would be far better listeners than the corrupted cookies who had heard her speak just minutes ago. She stepped forward. "If you're able, please look inside your respective house and ensure it hasn't been breached by one of the cookies. We need to be *certain* that Mr. Theo's cookie tins haven't been tampered with—other than the one Klaus and I already took care of, that is. If you see a cookie tin with a broken label, or with a label bearing a grey background and a reindeer rearing up to the right, alert your closest allies. We will need to dispose of it before sunrise."

Horace planted both hands firmly on top of his staff. "It will be done, Ms. Ginger."

"It will be done, Ms. Ginger," Klaus repeated to her. "There, that's taken care of. Shall we go?"

She nodded. "As quickly and quietly as a mouse."

CHAPTER 5
The Way the Cookie Crumbles

As soon as Ginger and Klaus had slipped under the window, they noticed that an unopened cookie tin was sitting on a side table beside a kitchen cabinet, and that Molasses was approaching it from above by swinging from one pendant light to another. How he had managed to get onto one of those lights in the first place, so close to the ceiling, Ginger could not guess. A respectable distance lay between them and their quarry; they were beside the kitchen sink, and the counter wrapped around the kitchen on three sides, with Molasses directly opposite of them. Nothing but cold kitchen tile stood in the void between the counters and cabinets.

"What's the plan?" Ginger whispered to Klaus.

"I was thinking I would just throw this huge knife as hard as I could at him," the mouse suggested. "That'd show him some sense."

"Klaus, that'll kill him!"

He considered that. "Yeah, you're probably right. Okay, what do you think we should do? He's your brother, after all."

"I—I think I should talk to him."

"That didn't work too well last time, you know."

"Last time, he had a crowd." She watched as Molasses landed beside the cookie tin. "This time, it's just us. But I *will* need your help getting up there."

"You've got it," he said. "Come on, follow me."

He led her past the sink and found that the owners of the home had conveniently placed an anti-fatigue mat on the nearby tile. He motioned toward it, and together they leapt down, their fall softened by the plush surface. They surveyed the living room right outside the kitchen and, seeing that there were no humans, scurried across the tile. It was only then that Molasses noticed them, and even with his permanent frosting smile, his frustration was evident to Ginger. He hopped once, twice, thrice—and with the ends of his arms he managed to partially remove the lid and tear the label on the cookie tin. With another leap, he grabbed onto the rim of the tin and hoisted himself up.

"Get ready to grab onto my tail!" said Klaus.

"I'm right behind you!" Ginger answered.

Klaus jumped high into the air, and Ginger clamped her arms around his tail while he was in mid-flight. His tiny claws burrowed into the wood of the side table, and he moved along its surface with blazing speed. Before Ginger knew it, they raced over the top and frightened Molasses in the process; the cookie was dipping one arm into his satchel for an armful of his fatal powder. He had been poised upon the thin metal of the cookie tin without a problem, but seeing his sister and a foreign mouse with body armor was apparently enough to cause him to wobble and try to regain his balance. Ginger wondered if that split half-second had spared the perfectly yummy batch of cookies—and those who would inevitably eat them—from a cruel fate.

She pushed herself into a standing position and took a moment to assess the situation. Molasses was balanced again on the edge of the tin, a wildness to his movements; she did not think it would take much to cause him to remove his arm from the satchel and spread the powder upon the cookies. But the fact that he was hesitating gave her hope. Maybe he *would* listen to reason, if only for a moment. A moment might be all that she needed.

"Who are you?" asked the gingerbread man, gesturing toward the knife-bearing rodent.

"I am called Klaus."

Molasses dropped his gesturing hand. "Klaus. Klaus the mouse. Are you serious?"

"The rhyme is...purely coincidental, I'm sure."

He looked back and forth between his sister and the mouse. Ginger wished she could tell what he was thinking. Was he weighing his options, wondering how he would manage to escape Klaus's vicious blade if he scattered the poison? Was he flummoxed by the fact that a cookie and a rodent were working together? Did he feel sorry for delivering his own sister up to a merciless army? Was he second-guessing the act of ruining Mr. Theo's creations and potentially harming the Sprinkletonians? She wished she knew—but even though he was her brother, their allegiances meant that they thought quite differently. She felt that there was a gulf between them, but she did not yet know if that gulf was as unbridgeable as it seemed.

She stepped toward Molasses, and Klaus reached toward the handle of his knife in case things went sideways. Molasses did not budge but continued to look back and forth between the two; it appeared that he was no closer to deciding his next course of action.

"Molasses," she said, "Brother, you don't have to do this. You don't."

"Why wouldn't I?" he asked her. Something in his voice begged a satisfactory answer to the question. "Who are these people to us? They are no one. What we *do* know is that they slighted Tanas, the one who enhanced us and opened our eyes to the truth. They hate him, Ginger, even though recognition—not hate—is what he deserves. We don't owe these people a thing."

"But we owe our maker *everything*," she reminded him. "He was the one who gave us life. We wouldn't even be here talking if it wasn't for Mr. Theo."

He shrugged. "Maybe you're right. And if that's the case, maybe you should blame Mr. Theo for all this. Blame *him* for everything that's happened."

"And what of our own responsibility—our responsibility to do what's right? Don't you realize our own hands in all this?" A figure of speech, of course, seeing as how gingerbread cookies did not have much in the way of hands. She hoped Molasses got the picture. "We agreed to be tools for Tanas to exact his vengeance on the people of Sprinkleton. He made us instruments of his rage. That doesn't come from a good place, Brother. He couldn't get what he wanted, so he infected a pair of perfectly good cookies to carry out his will. He is deceitful, spiteful, and envious. Can't you see that?"

Molasses paused, and Ginger was happy that he was at least taking the time to consider her words. He shifted on the edge of the tin. "Tanas's character is irrelevant. This is what I *feel* like doing, Sister. This is who I am, and nothing can change that."

She took another step forward. "Fine. Then let me ask you this: what you are doing—is it *good*?"

"Good?"

"Yes, Molasses. Are your deeds good?"

He turned his head to the left, and then to the right. "I—it's not—I mean, for me, they are good."

"That wasn't the question. Brother, are your deeds *good*—period?"

She hoped that she had presented the dilemma in a way that he understood. If he were to answer that what he was doing was good, then he would be claiming that it was good to cause harm to, and possibly kill, unsuspecting persons for a reason that was impossible to justify; if he answered that what he was doing was evil, then it was obvious that he should no longer proceed. He floundered there for a moment, unable to speak, and he appeared to Ginger like a cornered animal. Klaus's grip tightened on the handle of his knife.

"Brother?" said Ginger.

"If I were to stop," he told her, speaking slowly, "what would the others think of me? They would tease me and say that I wasn't able to finish what I started. I would be mocked for the rest of my days."

"To be fair, most of your peers are nothing but crumbs now," Klaus pointed out. "So there's that."

Ginger ignored that and looked into her brother's eyes. In many ways, he was the same cookie who had leapt off the baking sheet with her. She could not quit her pleading until he was safely back home. "You may be mocked, it's true. But isn't it worth it to live with a clear conscience before our dear Mr. Theo? Isn't *he* worth it?"

Molasses removed his hand from his satchel, and there was not a grain of powder to be seen on it. "But how—how can I get rid of this feeling? How can I stop wanting to do Tanas's bidding? It feels like it consumes every part of me."

Ginger walked up to the cookie tin and held out one arm. "Redemption is promised to those willing to reject the corruption within. Mr. Theo has the tools to get rid of Tanas's ingredients little by little. And one day, I believe those twisted ingredients will be gone altogether."

"Mr. Theo can really do that?" asked Molasses, his voice tender and hopeful.

"He can."

"How?"

Ginger chuckled. "He's the world's best baker. Is there anything he *can't* do?"

Molasses stood there for another few seconds, his body sometimes swinging closer to the cookies and sometimes closer to his sister. Then he seized the pirate hat on his head and cast it off the table, down into a small trash can at the foot of the nearest cabinet. He leaned forward and took hold of his sister's arm, and she pulled him down to the surface of the side table. He remained standing, but there was a sort of penitence to his posture. "I was too blind to see just how wrong my actions were. How did that happen?"

"Deception," said Ginger. "Whatever Tanas sprinkled on us is so potent that it can even convince us that bad things are good."

"That's terrifying," Klaus told them with a shudder. "I don't know this Tanas guy, but from everything I've heard, I can't say I'm all that fond of him."

Molasses clasped his other arm around Ginger's. "Sister...I'm so very sorry for being willing to hurt you. And I'm sorry for my deeds this evening. I would have continued on as I was had you not spoken up. I—I hope you can forgive me."

"I appreciate the sentiment, Brother," she said, "but in truth, I'm not the one you should be asking for forgiveness."

"Mr. Theo," he replied, nodding. "Do you think he can find it in his heart to forgive me?"

Ginger patted him on the back. "I'm sure of it. But you'll have to come with me back to his house to find out." She looked at Klaus, and then at her brother. "So what do you say, guys? Shall we go?"

As it turned out, the Colony Behind the Cabinets were most thorough in both their guarding of the fifteen homes and their ensuring that Mr. Theo's cookies remained safe for consumption. Some hours after sunrise, the report came to Klaus that no other Cookies of Tanas had entered the houses, and that all cookie tins were accounted for and untouched. Furthermore, so great was the defeat of the cookies that not a single one had been spotted after the conclusion of the scuffle; they were likely (so the report put it) "scattered throughout every corner of town and licking their wounds." The Colony showed additional faithfulness to their task by remaining at their posts well after sunrise, until every last human had woken from their slumber and gone into the living room to open presents. Many of the citizens had enjoyed their morning festivities, it was reported, with one or two of Mr. Theo's cookies in hand.

Ginger was informed that Tanas had not taken the news of his failure well, and upon hearing it, he had fled from Mr. Theo's house and left the town altogether. She was not sure whether to be elated or worried about the fact that the man was no longer lurking around the corner; he may no longer be *their* problem, but what was stopping him from conjuring a new malevolent plot on another town like Sprinkleton? And was there a guarantee that he would not return one day, perhaps with a desire to cause greater harm than before?

The Colony had returned to their shelter where, Klaus repeated to Ginger, they were safest for the time being. There they would await new orders from their king or remain in place until it was time to find a more permanent kingdom. Although Ginger asked Klaus whom they were hiding from, he refused to discuss it, only saying that he was not willing to speak ill of his pursuer. His voice resonated with respect and affection when he told her this, and she decided not to press him on the matter—for now.

Thankfully, Molasses was able to seek and receive forgiveness from his maker, and alongside the forgiveness came the promise of change. Mr. Theo took Ginger and Molasses into his kitchen and began a work on them to steadily remove the effects of Tanas's ingredients. It was not done without some degree of pain, and Ginger wondered if even her lifetime—the duration of which was something she could not even guess, as there was certainly no available literature on the lifecycle of a living cookie—would be long enough to fully remove the stain. But she trusted that the wise baker could and would do all that he had said, and fortunately, she did not have to believe alone; her brother was there with her again, not her enemy but an ally, and a recipient of the same promises.

It was midmorning on Christmas day when she and Molasses stepped out of Mr. Theo's house and onto a cliffside balcony overlooking Sprinkleton. Klaus had been waiting for them, sitting on a circular table beside a cherry-red wooden balustrade. A small ornamental Christmas tree stood just a few inches away from him, the centerpiece of the table. As soon as he heard the door creak open, he turned to look at the two cookies, and he began to sniff the air.

"By my whiskers!" he exclaimed, his tail whipping behind him. "I don't know what Mr. Theo did to you two, but that rosemary aroma is...milder, somehow. Not that you two were *smelly*, per se, but...well, rosemary just doesn't complement gingerbread, you know?"

"Bless your nose, Klaus," Ginger said with a giggle. "I'll have to take your word for it."

She and Molasses managed to reach the tabletop by hopping from a planter to a chair and finally to the table. The view of Sprinkleton was breathtaking, even in the brightness of day. A thin layer of snow was feathered across every red roof, the quaint front yards glistened from the morning slush, unobstructed windows served as frames for scintillating Christmas trees and rejoicing families, chimneys belched out columns of smoke, and neighbors greeted each other while taking morning walks or dawdling in their yards. The view closer to Mr. Theo's house was even more beautiful, if that were possible: pine trees reached up from the hillside in an attempt to touch the sky, ice still coating their viridescent needles; songbirds were perched on many boughs, celebrating the day with their trilling melodies; patches of snow made the slope leading down to the town appear as a giant chessboard. Ginger was not quite sure where it was coming from, but she heard Christmas music jingling gently all around her.

Klaus, now leaning on his paring knife, studied the gingerbread man for a moment. "So how do you feel, Molasses?" he asked.

"Like a brand-new cookie," was his answer. There was a novel joy in his voice. "I have Mr. Theo to thank for that. But also...I must thank you. Thank you both for seeking me when I didn't want to be found. And thank *you,* Mr. Klaus." He bowed to the best of his ability. "For you took on my sister's burden as your own and protected her from my stupidity."

"It was no burden," said Klaus, bowing in return. "Your sister is one-of-a-kind. Her love for you, for the Sprinkletonians, and for Mr. Theo is admirable. It was an honor to join her on this Christmas adventure, and to serve however I was able."

Molasses sighed. "I suppose the only thing that would make this day better would be the exchanging of gifts, the way the humans do it. But alas! The three of us were far too preoccupied to prepare gifts."

"Gifts can be nice," said Ginger, "but what I've learned today is that Christmas is not about the shiny and costly things—not really."

Molasses looked at her. "What *is* it about?"

She turned to Klaus. "It's about self-sacrifice, the way Klaus was willing to risk his own life so that I might succeed in my mission to find you. And it's about realizing that we aren't capable of removing the corruption within ourselves; only our creator can do that. It's okay—in fact, it's necessary—to lean on the one who made us."

Klaus drew in a sharp whistle and poked the ground with the claws on his feet. "Christmas is not about shiny things, eh? Really? Well then, this is awkward."

Ginger threw one arm to her head. "Oh no. Klaus, what did you do?"

"Nothing significant! But you guys were in Mr. Theo's house for a while, and I didn't quite know what to do with myself all that time. So I went exploring and found a little something for Molasses."

"For Molasses?" Ginger pouted. "Not for your old friend Ginger?"

"I thought you said Christmas wasn't about gifts." Klaus smirked. "Anyway, being the negotiator of our group, you wouldn't really care for this."

Ginger crossed her arms and thought it would be justified if she did not speak to present company for at least ten minutes. Klaus moved away stealthily and disappeared behind the decorative Christmas tree on the table. When he reemerged, he was wielding a large kitchen utensil. Its size was disproportionate to his body (even more so than his paring knife), but it looked to be a perfect fit for Molasses.

"A fine new mace for a fine new ally," he said to the gingerbread man.

"Klaus, that's a whisk for mixing cookie batter," Ginger told him, putting one arm to her head. "It's not a weapon."

"Well, it *could* be a weapon in the right arms." He beamed at his new friend. "My guess is that Tanas dropped it in his frenzied retreat, the clumsy oaf. If you're willing,

Molasses, I could use another warrior by my side in the fight to come."

Molasses grabbed the handle of the whisk without words but with a small bow and reverence for the significance of the moment. He swung it a few times and seemed very impressed with its ability to clobber the air.

Ginger rubbed the back of her head. "Just what fight are you talking about, Klaus?"

The mouse turned away from them and gazed at the town. "The corruption of Tanas remains on those few cookies who survived the battle. I saw the fight in their eyes. To them, this defeat is only temporary." He gave Ginger a solemn stare. "At some point they will try to even the score. And we must be ready for them."

"We will be," Ginger assured him. "But for now, let's enjoy this Christmas together. Molasses is back, and the villagers below, other than one unfortunate family, are enjoying Mr. Theo's cookies." She smiled, but then again, she was *always* smiling. "I can't think of a better ending."

THE
END

Made in the USA
Las Vegas, NV
14 December 2023

82754072R00028